FamilyFun Cooking

By Deanna F. Cook
and the Experts at FamilyFun Magazine

New York

This book is dedicated to
the readers of *FamilyFun* magazine

Copyright © 2002 Disney Enterprises, Inc.
All rights reserved. No part of this book may be used or reproduced in any manner whatsoever without the written permission of the Publisher. Printed in the United States of America. For information address Disney Editions, 114 Fifth Avenue, New York, NY, 10011.

Most of the recipes and photographs in this book were previously published in *FamilyFun* magazine. These pages were excerpted from *FamilyFun Cookbook*.

FamilyFun magazine is a division of Disney Publishing Worldwide.
To order a subscription, call 800-289-4849.

FamilyFun Magazine
BOOK EDITORS: Alexandra Kennedy, Deanna F. Cook, and Katherine Eastman
PRODUCTION EDITOR: Paula Noonan
RECIPE TESTERS: Cynthia Caldwell, Vivi Mannuzza
PRODUCTION DIRECTOR: Jennifer Mayer
PRODUCTION ASSISTANT: Martha Jenkins

Impress, Inc.
DESIGNERS: Hans Teensma and James McDonald
PHOTO AND ART ASSOCIATE: Tobye Cook
ASSISTANT DESIGNER: Leslie Tane

The staffs of **FamilyFun** and **Impress, Inc.**
conceived and produced *FamilyFun Cooking* at
244 Main Street, Northampton, MA 01060

In collaboration with
Disney Editions, 114 Fifth Avenue, New York, NY, 10011

Pre-press Production by Aurora Graphics, Portsmouth, NH
Printed in Hong Kong by Wing King Tong Co. Ltd.

Library of Congress Cataloging-in-Publication Data on file

ISBN 0-7868-5415-4

Contents

Plain and Simple Roast Chicken: *Page 30*

1 **Getting Ready** 4 *Learn how to turn mealtime into a satisfying family gathering*

2 **Breakfast: Rise & Shine** 8 *Winning recipes that make the most important meal of the day the most delicious meal of the day ∼ Eggs ... 8 ... Pancakes & Waffles ... 10 ... Muffins ... 12*

3 **Lunch Specials** 14 *Shake up the lunch-box routine with creative ideas your kids won't eighty-six in the cafeteria ∼ Sandwiches ... 14 ... Hot Lunches ... 17*

4 **After-School Snacks** 20 *Secrets for the afternoon tide-over ∼ Sweets Snacks ... 20 ... Crunchy Snacks ... 24 .*

5 **Dinner's Ready** 26 *No more cooking three dinners a night! Discover meals for fussy eaters, young and old ∼ Meats ... 27 ... Poultry ... 30 ... Fish & Seafood ... 32 ... Pasta ... 34*

6 **Side Dishes** 36 *Bring out the fun in the healthy dishes that round out every meal ∼ Vegetables ... 36 ... Rices & Grains ... 38 ... Potatoes ... 40*

Scrambled Eggs with Tomato and Basil: *Page 9*

7 **Can I Have Dessert?** 42 *Grand finales, from playful cookies to cakes for special occasions ∼ Cookies ... 42 ... Cakes ... 46*

Sandwiches: *Page 14*

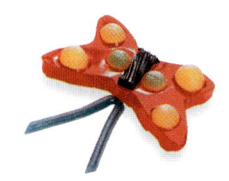

Fluttery Creations: *Page 21*

Getting Ready

As the food editor of *FamilyFun* magazine, I like to root around in our file cabinets and pull out letters from our readers whenever I need a boost. Hearing a parent thank us for the recipes in the magazine is satisfying, but looking at a child's expression in the accompanying photo — holding up a Father's Day cake or a homemade apple pie — makes my day. A child's excitement as he offers up a slightly lopsided creation is proof that cooking is about family, about making something good to eat in the kitchen, and sharing it with someone you love. Forget the flowers — say it with spaghetti and cupcakes.

Since we started *FamilyFun* in 1991, families have come to rely on us for our cooking tips and recipes. They've clipped and saved and spilled flour all over them — the mark of good recipes. We decided it was about time to gather our most popular recipes in one place for the busy parents who want to put good meals on the table and enjoy them with their kids. In this cookbook, you will find recipes for real food, meals parents actually make and kids actually eat. And they're fun, from the preparation to the table.

Over the years, our contributors and readers have shared their tricks for satisfying every eater at the table. I am relieved to report that none of them involve preparing a different meal for each family member — a strategy some exasperated parents resort to. A couple of the tricks appeal particularly to kids. For starters, the names of the recipes are clever. This may be a small point to an adult,

but to many a picky child a catchy name makes a meal more appetizing. An innovative presentation is also key to making food more tempting. We won't pretend that every mom and dad has time to carve radishes into flowers, but some simple tricks — cutting sandwiches with cookie cutters, arranging sliced fruit into faces, or serving fun pasta shapes — win over the kindergarten set.

If you have finicky eaters in your household (and who doesn't?) you can still present nutritionally balanced meals. For the child who turns up his nose to a tomato slice tucked in a grilled-cheese sandwich, for example, we say offer him a host of healthful add-ins — avocado, salsa, onion, broccoli. After all, things taste better when you have a choice.

Try to expand your repertoire in other ways as well. When I was a kid, the most exotic thing my family ate was Swedish meatballs. Now we can't imagine a week without stir-fry. The trend is that families are eating out more and tasting new flavors all over town: Mexican, Chinese, Japanese, Thai, Italian, Greek, Caribbean. As our palates become more sophisticated — more receptive to a broad range of ingredients and cooking methods — we are expanding our choices. Grocery stores have responded, too, with shelves stocked with fresh herbs, specialty vegetables, and seafoods unheard of a generation ago. This recipe collection takes advantage of our global education with simple-to-follow recipes that can easily be made in your own kitchen.

When you're preparing meals, keep in mind that the kitchen is the family room — the core of the home, where everyone gravitates, not just for eating, but for learning and growing as a family. We hope these recipes will bring your family as many happy memories in the kitchen as they have brought the readers of *FamilyFun*. Now get ready to share some deliciously good times.

Eat dinner together. For many busy families, the evening meal is is a good time to share ideas, catch up on news, and enjoy each other's company, and it may be the only time your kids get your undivided attention. Make sure the television is off and that all phone calls will be returned after dinner is over. At the table, the best family entertainment can happen spontaneously through storytelling, laughter, and the appreciation of a good meal shared.

Plan menus ahead. An hour spent planning meals on a Sunday will save you time all week long. Brainstorm new recipe ideas with your kids and involve them in the selection process; kids who participate in menu planning are more likely to eat the meals. Be sure that each meal is complete — with a protein, grain, vegetable, and dessert. When you have a menu, you can compile a grocery list and avoid daily trips to the market.

Raise healthy eaters. The key to good nutrition is not counting every calorie or avoiding all fatty foods: It's eating small portions of a variety of foods. In other words, it's okay to serve your child a cupcake as long as you also serve a healthy sandwich, carrot sticks, and a glass of milk. Be sure to set a good example by eating healthy foods yourself.

Introduce new foods. Taste is a learned behavior. It's tempting to serve pizza seven nights of the week, but it's more important to educate your children's palates so they can learn to love a wide range of foods. Introduce a new fruit or vegetable on a regular basis, and if your children don't like it, reintroduce it a few months later. Kids' tastes change over time.

Teach your kids to cook. Learning to cook is an important life skill and a great hobby to get your kids hooked on. Encourage your kids to be creative in the kitchen — to smell fresh herbs and decide whether to add them to the soup, for example — and to enjoy the process of making something to eat.

Designer Table Setting

In *FamilyFun* reader Nancy Weber's household, table setting is transformed from a chore into an art form. The person setting the table gets to set it any way he or she sees fit — as long as four people can dine with the result. Sometimes they have plates under the chairs and all the knives and forks in a pile in the middle of the table; other times they have origami napkin swans; sometimes everyone has a different shape and color glass, and the napkins are tied around the rungs of the chairs. And one night Dad made a model of the starship *Enterprise* using forks, knives, and plates.

Step 1. Arrange a napkin on the diagonal and pull one layer down.

Step 2. Flip the napkin over and fold in the two sides.

Step 3. Turn it over again and fill with silverware.

Getting Ready

Eggs

Sunday Morning Omelets

Kids like to choose their own fillings for this classic egg dish. Encourage them to invent combinations from whatever leftover vegetables, spreads, cheeses, and meats you have on hand. How about a jelly and cream cheese omelet?

- ½ tablespoon butter or margarine
- 2 eggs
- 1 tablespoon water
- Salt and pepper to taste

Filling options:
- 1 tablespoon grated cheese, such as Cheddar or Mozzarella
- 1 tablespoon cottage cheese, Boursin, or flavored cream cheese (see page 35)
- 2 tablespoons diced, cooked chicken
- 1 tablespoon crispy bacon pieces
- 2 teaspoons jam or jelly
- 2 sliced mushrooms
- 2 cherry tomato halves
- 1 tablespoon diced green or red pepper
- 1 tablespoon diced onion

In a large, nonstick frying pan, melt the butter or margarine over medium-high heat. Beat the eggs with a fork in a small bowl and stir in the water, salt, and pepper. Pour the egg mixture over the butter, swirling the egg until you have coated the pan with a thin layer of uncooked egg. Sprinkle the desired fillings over the omelet and cook for 1 to 3 more minutes, or until desired doneness. To serve, hold the pan at a 45-degree angle and, with a spatula, gently fold the omelet in half. Makes 1 generous omelet.

Breakfast Burrito

The morning after a Mexican meal, I use up my leftover tortillas, grated cheese, chopped onion, and salsa in this delicious roll-up sandwich.

- 1 tablespoon butter
- 6 eggs, beaten
- 4 to 6 8-inch flour tortillas

Filling options:
- ½ cup grated Monterey Jack cheese
- 1 plum tomato, chopped
- 1 small onion, diced
- ¼ green or red pepper, chopped
- ½ avocado, diced
- Salsa
- Sliced olives

Over medium-high heat, melt the butter in a large, nonstick frying pan and scramble and cook the eggs to your liking. Meanwhile, warm the tortillas for a few minutes on the rack of a 250° oven, then fill with the egg and your choice of ingredients. Fold into a burrito (see page 159 for directions). Serves 4.

Breakfast Burrito

Egg Heads

For a silly activity that makes terrific use of eggshells, you can make Egg Heads with wild grass-dos. For each, you'll need a raw egg, a needle, grass seed, and potting soil. First, use the needle to make a hole about the size of a quarter in one end of an egg, then drain the contents and rinse out the shell. Gently draw or paint faces on the shell and set in an egg carton to dry. Spoon soil into the shell, then plant the grass seeds according to package instructions. Moisten, cover with plastic wrap, and place in a sunny window until the seeds sprout — about one week. When the Egg Heads have a thick head of hair, remove the covering and style with scissors. Water your Egg Heads regularly.

FamilyFun COOKING

Scrambled Eggs with Cream Cheese and Chives

Learning to scramble eggs is a great cooking lesson for kids. Fresh chives and cream cheese create a creamy embellishment.

- 1 tablespoon butter or margarine
- 2 eggs
- 1 to 2 tablespoons cream cheese, cut into ½-inch cubes
- 4 fresh chives, snipped into pieces

Melt the butter in a small saucepan over medium heat. Beat the eggs, pour into the pan, and stir for 1 minute. Add the cream cheese and chives and cook to desired doneness. Serves 1.

Cottage Cheese and Dill:
Add 1 heaping tablespoon cottage cheese and 2 teaspoons chopped fresh dill (or 1 teaspoon dried dill) to 2 nearly cooked scrambled eggs.

Cheddar Cheese and Bacon:
While stirring, sprinkle 1 to 2 pieces of cooked, crumbled bacon and 2 teaspoons grated Cheddar cheese into scrambled eggs. Let the cheese melt before serving.

Tomato and Basil:
Toss half a small, diced tomato and 1 to 2 teaspoons chopped fresh basil into your scrambled eggs before serving.

Salsa, Cilantro, and Sour Cream:
Mix 1 to 2 tablespoons salsa, 1 teaspoon chopped fresh cilantro, and 2 teaspoons sour cream into scrambled eggs while cooking.

GREEN EGGS & HAM, I AM, I AM

To celebrate Dr. Seuss's birthday, kick off March 2nd by reading *Green Eggs & Ham* and whipping up a batch of green scrambled eggs. Just add a few drops of green food coloring to your family recipe.

Variations on Scrambled Eggs (clockwise from bottom left):
- Tomato and Basil
- Cheddar Cheese and Bacon
- Cream Cheese and Chives
- Salsa, Cilantro, and Sour Cream
- Cottage Cheese and Dill

Breakfast: Rise and Shine

Sunday Waffles

Pancakes & Waffles

The Perfect Pancake Mix

FamilyFun contributor Becky Okrent developed this vitamin-packed mix to encourage her family to make pancakes in short order.

- 3 cups all-purpose flour
- 3 teaspoons baking soda
- 4½ teaspoons baking powder
- 1½ teaspoons salt
- 1 tablespoon sugar (optional)
- 2 cups whole wheat or oat flour, or a combination
- 1 cup seven whole grain cereal (available at health food stores)
- 1 cup cornmeal
- 4 tablespoons wheat germ (optional)

In a large mixing bowl, sift the all-purpose flour with the baking soda, baking powder, salt, and optional sugar. Drop in the remaining flour, cereal, cornmeal, and wheat germ and stir until thoroughly blended. Store in an airtight container and, if using wheat germ, refrigerate. Makes 7½ cups, enough for 15 batches of 5 pancakes.

Perfect Pancakes:

You can store leftover batter in the refrigerator for two days and reheat leftover pancakes in a toaster.

- 1 tablespoon butter
- 1 egg
- ½ cup nonfat yogurt, buttermilk, sour cream, or milk
- ½ cup Perfect Pancake Mix

Set a griddle or skillet over medium heat and melt the butter. Lightly beat the egg with the yogurt, buttermilk, sour cream, or milk. Add the pancake mix and stir just until smooth.

Ladle the batter onto the skillet. Turn the pancakes when you see air bubbles on the surface (about 1 minute). Serve with maple syrup, jam, yogurt, or confectioners' sugar. Makes about 5 medium pancakes.

Perfect Blueberry Pancakes:

Stir ½ cup fresh or frozen blueberries into the batter before cooking.

Sunday Waffles

The leisurely pace of Sundays means extra time for *FamilyFun* contributor Becky Okrent and her family to make waffles, using her Perfect Pancake Mix.

- 2 eggs, separated
- 1 cup milk
- 3 tablespoons vegetable oil or melted butter
- 1 cup Perfect Pancake Mix

In a bowl, combine the egg yolks, milk, and oil or butter. Stir in the Perfect Pancake Mix. Beat the egg whites until stiff and gently fold into the batter. Cook on a greased waffle iron until lightly browned. Makes 4 to 6 waffles.

Perfect Blueberry Pancakes

Breakfast: Rise and Shine

Muffins

Good Morning Muffins and Best Apple Butter

Hot Mulled Apple Cider

Combine a gallon of cider with 4 cinnamon sticks, a few cloves, ¼ teaspoon of ground nutmeg, and several orange slices. Gently warm over medium heat. Strain and transfer to mugs. For extra flavor, add a cinnamon stick and orange slice to each serving.

Good Morning Muffins

Thanks to these nutritious muffins, my brother gets his kids to eat apples and carrots for breakfast.

- 3 eggs
- ½ cup sugar
- ½ cup vegetable oil
- 1 cup grated apples
- 1 cup grated carrots
- 1 cup whole wheat flour
- 1 cup all-purpose flour
- 1 tablespoon baking powder
- ¼ teaspoon salt
- 1 teaspoon cinnamon

Preheat the oven to 375°. Lightly grease a 12-cup muffin tin or line it with paper liners and set aside. Blend the eggs, sugar, and oil until well combined. Stir in the grated apples and carrots. In a separate bowl, sift the flours, baking powder, salt, and cinnamon. Blend the dry ingredients with the apple mixture until just combined. Spoon the batter into the muffin tins and bake for 25 minutes, or until golden brown. Makes 12 muffins.

Best Apple Butter

As I learned from my mother, who created this recipe, the best part of making apple butter is that your house fills with a sweet, cinnamon aroma. It isn't a lot of work, but it takes a long time to bake, so plan to make it when you are working around the house. Nothing is better when spread on muffins, scones, or toast.

- 9 to 10 apples, peeled, cored, and cut into 1-inch chunks
- 1 cup apple cider
- 2 teaspoons apple pie spice (available in the spice rack at your grocer's)

Place the apples in a large, nonreactive saucepan with the cider. Cover the pot and cook for about 30 minutes over low heat, or until the apples are soft. Cool, divide into two batches, and puree each in the bowl of a food processor or blender. Pour all of the pureed fruit into a 13- by 9- by 2-inch baking dish, sprinkle with the apple pie spice, and stir well.

Stirring every 20 minutes, bake in a preheated 300° oven for 2 to 3 hours, or until your apple butter is deep brown and thick. Cool and then scoop it into a clean jar with a sealable lid. It will keep for up to 2 months in your refrigerator. Makes 1½ cups.

P B & J Surprise Muffins

The inspiration of *FamilyFun* contributor Beth Hillson, these moist peanut butter muffins hide a secret jelly or jam filling. She lets her son pick the flavor and puts him in charge of spooning the surprise into the batter. Her advice: Make a batch on a Sunday so your child can enjoy them as breakfast treats all week long.

- 1¾ cups all-purpose flour
- ⅓ cup sugar
- 2½ teaspoons baking powder
- ½ teaspoon salt
- ½ cup creamy peanut butter
- 1 large egg
- ¾ cup milk
- ⅓ cup butter, melted
- ½ cup strawberry, raspberry, or grape jelly or jam

Preheat the oven to 375°. Line a 12-cup muffin tin with paper liners. In a large bowl, combine the flour, sugar, baking powder, and salt. In a separate bowl, mix the peanut butter with the egg; add the milk, a little at a time, then add the butter. Mix well. Pour the wet batter into the bowl with the dry ingredients and stir gently to combine (the batter will be stiff).

Put a heaping tablespoon of batter in the bottom of each muffin cup. Use a finger to make an indentation in the center and put a teaspoon of jelly in the hole. Cover with another heaping tablespoon of batter, or enough to fill each cup about two thirds full. Spread the top batter gently until no jelly is visible. Bake for 20 minutes, then turn the muffins onto a wire baking rack to cool. Be careful — the jelly centers can get hot. Makes 12 muffins.

Breakfast: Rise and Shine

Sandwiches

Something Fishy

Even picky preschoolers won't throw back this clever lunch. Serve it with Goldfish crackers and gummy worms.

- 2 slices whole wheat or white bread
- 1 6-ounce can tuna in water, drained
- 2 tablespoons mayonnaise
  Lettuce
- 1 tomato, thinly sliced

Stack the bread slices and cut out the fish shape below, or use a fish-shaped cookie cutter. Make a tuna salad with the tuna and mayonnaise, then layer it with the lettuce and tomato. Serves 1.

PB and Jellyfish:

For variety, try a peanut butter and jelly sandwich on the precut, fish-shaped bread.

Mini Muffuletta

Salami fans always order up this smaller take on the New Orleans classic.

- 1 small hard roll
- 2 slices salami
- 2 slices ham
- 1 slice provolone
  Diced onion (optional)
  Sliced olives (optional)
  Sliced radishes (optional)
  Olive oil
  Vinegar

Cut the roll in half and place the salami, ham, and provolone on the bread. Add the onion, olives, and radishes, if desired. Drizzle the bread with olive oil and a splash of vinegar (too much will make it soggy). Serves 1.

Easy Lunch-box Stuffers

- Carrots, celery sticks, or broccoli florets with a small container of salad dressing for dipping. (To prevent the veggies from drying out, wrap them in a damp paper towel.)
- Fresh fruit: Try sliced apples rubbed with lemon juice, fresh or canned pineapple chunks, melon in season, fruit salad, or a fruit smoothie.
- Pretzels, salted peanuts, or popcorn
- Celery sticks filled with cream cheese or peanut butter and raisins
- Fruit yogurt packed in a thermos
- Crackers served plain or sandwiched with peanut butter, jelly, or cheese
- Mozzarella sticks or string cheese
- Graham crackers, plain or sandwiched with peanut butter
- Dried fruit: Raisins, apricots, apples, or pineapples
- Tortilla chips with a small jar of salsa
- Pasta salad or soup in a thermos
- Pickles, olives, or hard-boiled eggs
- Stickers or a note from you

Something Fishy

Sailboat Sandwiches

Sailboat Sandwiches

These novel sandwiches — filled with tuna salad and topped with Cheddar cheese sails — give kids a real feel for the seashore. Set these treats in a plateful of blue corn tortilla chips to complete the nautical theme.

- 4 dinner rolls
- 1 cup tuna salad
- 4 slices Cheddar cheese
- 8 toothpicks

Slice the tops off the dinner rolls and hollow them out. Fill the rolls with the tuna salad or any other filling your kids like. Slice the Cheddar cheese into rectangles about ⅛ inch thick and cut the rectangles on the diagonal to make triangles. Insert a toothpick into each triangle to make little sails and add them to the top of your "boats." Makes 4.

Veggies in a Blanket

The young *FamilyFun* readers Ian and Abigail Rowswell entered this burrito-like concoction in our Kids' Snack-off Contest, and their recipe got rave reviews. The siblings, ages nine and six, from Medina, New York, say the sandwich is kind of like a wrapped-up salad.

- 2 6-inch flour tortillas
- 2 tablespoons cream cheese
- 1 medium carrot, grated
- 2 lettuce leaves

Wrap each tortilla in a paper towel and microwave for 15 seconds (or warm in a cast-iron pan on low). Spread 1 tablespoon cream cheese over each tortilla, add carrot and lettuce, and roll. Makes 2.

SPROUT YOUR OWN

For a healthy crunch on your child's sandwich, try this indoor gardening project. Measure ½ cup of dried beans (alfalfa, radish, wheat berry, mung, lentil, or adzuki) into a 2-quart, widemouthed plastic jar. Cover with nylon mesh or cheesecloth and secure with a rubber band. Fill halfway with cool water and set the jar away from direct sunlight for 8 hours. Gently drain the water through the mesh cover and return the jar to its shady spot. Twice a day for the next three days, fill the jar with tepid water, drain the water, then set the jar back in the shade. By the fifth day, your crop should be ready to harvest. Your sprout growers need only to reach into the jar and gently pull out handfuls of the mature sprouts. Toss them with salad dressing or stuff them into a sandwich and enjoy. To store leftover sprouts, wrap them in a double thickness of paper towel and refrigerate in a plastic bag.

Lunch Specials

Peanut Puzzler

Peanut Butter & Banana Bread Sandwich

Banana bread is the secret ingredient in this twist on the old standby.

- 2 slices of banana bread
   Peanut butter
- 1 banana or apple, sliced

Spread peanut butter on one slice of banana bread. Layer with the banana or apple slices and top with the second bread slice. In a matter of seconds, you've put together a nutritious sandwich that has a sweet dessert flavor. Serves 1.

Peanut Butter and...

Even the most devoted PB & J fans enjoy a little variety. Try combining one of the following ingredients with peanut butter for a novel sandwich.

- Sliced bananas or apples
- Fresh berries
- Maple syrup
- Crispy bacon
- Raisins, dried apricots, or dried apple rings
- Chopped, pitted dates
- Grated carrots
- Wheat germ and honey
- Apple butter

Peanut Puzzler

This spread is great with fresh fruit, such as a few halved grapes, apple slices, or banana slices. For added enticement, you can use a cookie cutter to shape the sandwich into puzzle pieces.

- 1 cup peanut butter, creamy or chunky
- 3 tablespoons toasted sesame seeds
- ¼ cup honey

Mix together all the ingredients and spread on bread or fruit. Makes 1¼ cups.

Fun Fact
The average American child will eat 1,500 peanut butter sandwiches by high school graduation.

Personalized Lunch Bags

Pick up reusable, nylon lunch bags and some bright puffy paints at a discount or craft supply store and let your kids decorate their own lunch bags. Chances are there will be no mistaking whose lunch is inside.

FamilyFun COOKING

Hot Lunches

Grilled-Cheese Sandwich: The Next Generation

Grilled-Cheese Sandwich: The Next Generation

This sandwich from *FamilyFun* contributor Mollie Katzen is a far cry from the grilled cheese on buttered white of our youths. Open-faced and open to experimentation, this healthy lunch is a favorite in her household.

- ½ cup olive oil
- 1 small red onion, chopped
- 1 medium stalk broccoli, in small florets
- Salt to taste
- Dried thyme
- 8 slices sourdough, rye, or wheat bread
- 2 cups grated Cheddar cheese

Heat 2 tablespoons of the olive oil in a frying pan over medium heat and wait 30 seconds. Add the onions and cook for 2 minutes. Add the broccoli, sprinkle with salt and 2 pinches of thyme, and cook, stirring, for 8 to 10 minutes. Transfer the vegetables to a bowl and set aside.

Using a pastry brush, paint the bread slices lightly on both sides with the remaining olive oil (a good job for kids). Heat the pan on medium-low, add a few bread slices, and cook until golden brown. Flip the bread and reduce the heat to low. Place a small pile of broccoli florets and chopped onion on the center of each piece of bread. Sprinkle cheese over the vegetables and cover the pan until the cheese melts. Let the cheese cool a bit before serving. Serves 4.

Lunch Specials

Designosaur a Pizza

FunFact
When the Earl of Sandwich ordered meat brought to him between two slices of bread, he inadvertently invented the lunch-box standby.

Designosaur a Pizza

Young *FamilyFun* reader Jacob Sandmire of Sandy, Utah, gets such a kick out of helping his mom make dinosaur-shaped pizzas that he forgets the vegetables he's using for eyes and mouths are destined to be eaten. By the time the pizzas are done, the veggies are buried under melted cheese, and Jacob's raring to dig in. (Many grocers sell bread dough in the frozen food section, or you can make your own from scratch.)

- 2 pounds bread dough
- 1 large dinosaur cookie cutter (available at kitchen supply and and craft stores)

Toppings:
- ½ cup pizza or spaghetti sauce
- ½ cup grated carrots
- ½ cup steamed broccoli florets
- 1½ to 2 cups grated mix of Colby and Monterey Jack cheeses
- ½ cup chopped ham or pepperoni
- ½ cup chopped green pepper
- ½ to 1 cup sliced black olives
- ½ cup chopped onions
- ½ cup sliced mushrooms
- ½ cup chopped tomatoes

Preheat the oven to 350°. Roll out, stretch, and press the dough ¼-inch thick, then cut it into dinosaurs. Line up the shapes on a lightly greased cookie sheet and let your kids spread on the sauce and toppings of their choice. Make eyes, mouths, and spikes down the backs with larger olive pieces. Bake for 15 to 20 minutes, or until the edges lightly brown. Makes 8 mini pizzas.

Croque Monsieur

For a welcome change to the everyday grilled cheese, try this classic French alternative.

- 2 slices wheat bread
- 2 teaspoons butter
- 2 slices American cheese
- 1 slice ham

Spread butter on one side of each piece of bread. In a frying pan over medium-low heat, place one piece of bread, butter side down, then layer with cheese, ham, then cheese. Top with the remaining slice of bread and grill until the cheese melts and the bread is lightly browned. Flip the sandwich over to brown the other side. Serves 1.

GRILLED CHEESE AND...

Jazz up your grilled cheese with the following:
- Sliced tomatoes
- Salsa
- Sliced onions
- Fresh dill or basil
- Sliced apple
- Sliced green pepper
- Grated carrot
- Finely diced cucumber
- Olives

Try some different cheeses for a whole new flavor:
- Mozzarella
- Brie
- Monterey Jack
- Muenster
- Swiss

FamilyFun COOKING

Turkey Meatball Sub

For a low-fat alternative to the traditional meatball sub, try this turkey version. It will stand up to a slathering of tomato sauce, onions, peppers, and melted Mozzarella cheese.

Meatballs:
- 1 pound ground turkey
- 1 egg, beaten
- ¼ cup minced onion
- 1 teaspoon oregano
- 1 teaspoon basil
- Salt and pepper to taste
- 3 tablespoons bread crumbs

Subs:
- 3 to 4 sub rolls
- 1 small onion, sliced and sautéed (optional)
- 1 green pepper, sliced and sautéed (optional)
- 2 cups tomato sauce
- 1½ cups grated Mozzarella cheese (optional)

Preheat your oven to 350°. In a large bowl, break up the turkey meat. Blend the egg with the onions, oregano, basil, and salt and pepper and thoroughly mix into the turkey. Sprinkle with bread crumbs and mix. Roll the meat into 2-inch balls and bake on a jelly roll pan for about 25 minutes, turning occasionally until light brown and completely cooked. (Alternatively, you can pan-brown the 2-inch balls in a lightly oiled, large skillet, turning them until completely cooked. Drain on paper towels.)

To build a sub, set two to three meatballs into a roll and layer on the sautéed onion and green pepper. Spread with the tomato sauce and top with the grated Mozzarella. Warm in the oven until the cheese melts and then serve. Makes 3 to 4 subs.

Lunch Specials

Pizza Men

These two cheery designs are offered as a suggestion, not a blueprint — children tend to be inventive when creating faces! (See the recipe for Designosaur a Pizza, opposite, for other topping options that may inspire your kids.)

- 2 tablespoons tomato sauce
- 1 English muffin, split and toasted
- ⅓ to ¼ cup grated Mozzarella cheese
- 3 olives, cut in half
- 1 slice red pepper
- 1 slice green pepper

Spread tomato sauce on both English muffin halves. Sprinkle grated cheese all over one half. Add olive halves for eyes and a nose, and a red pepper slice for a mouth. On the other muffin half, use olive slices for eyes and a nose, a green pepper for a mouth, and the remaining cheese for hair. Broil in a toaster oven for 5 minutes. Makes 2 individual pizzas.

Pizza Men

How To Make Bread Crust Croutons

Don't toss those crusts — they make great croutons. Each day, place them into a sealable bag and store it in the refrigerator. At the end of the week, cube the collection of crusts, toss them with melted butter, and arrange them on a baking sheet. Sprinkle with herbs, such as oregano, parsley, and paprika. Bake in a 350° oven for 20 minutes, or until the crusts are lightly toasted. Serve over fresh green salad or as a soup garnish.

Sweet Snacks

Choc-o-bananas

Choc-o-bananas

With no stove-top cooking or chopping required, this frozen banana recipe is truly for children. The chocolate hardens quickly, so work fast.

- 3 bananas
- 6 Popsicle sticks
- 3 1.5-ounce chocolate bars
- 1 tablespoon nut topping, crispy rice cereal, granola, or shredded coconut (optional)

Peel the bananas and remove any stringy fibers. Cut them in half, widthwise, and push a Popsicle stick through the cut end of each half. Cover them in plastic wrap and freeze for about 3 hours.

Place the chocolate bars in a microwave-proof bowl and cook on high for about 2 minutes, or until the chocolate melts (check after 1 minute). Stir in the nuts, cereal, or coconut. Using a butter knife, spread the chocolate mixture over the frozen bananas to coat them completely. Kids can roll them in more topping, but this is messy! Rest the pops on a plate covered with waxed paper and freeze until ready to serve. These keep in the freezer for 1 to 2 weeks. Makes 6.

Delectable Dominoes

Kids won't bother adding up the dots on these edible game pieces before popping them down the hatch. Spread graham crackers with a thin layer of cream cheese or peanut butter, then arrange chocolate, butterscotch, and white chocolate chip dots in domino patterns.

Chocolate Quicksand

There is really no need to measure the chocolate for this — just squirt to taste.

- 1 banana, peeled
- 1 cup vanilla or chocolate ice cream or frozen yogurt
- ½ cup milk
- ¼ cup chocolate syrup

In the morning, slice the banana, place it in a plastic lunch bag, and freeze. After school, place all the ingredients in a blender and process until smooth. Makes 1½ cups.

An Edible Fishbowl

Dig up that old fishbowl and give it a good scrub. Then try this "sea" food that Sandy Drummond and Betsy Rhein of Holland, Michigan, adapted from a creative Jell-O advertisement.

- 6 3-ounce packages of blueberry gelatin dessert
- 1 cup blueberries or grapes
   Gummy fish

Prepare the blueberry gelatin in a large mixing bowl according to package directions and refrigerate until partially set (for an aquarium with more waves, let the gelatin thoroughly set). Make a rocky ocean floor by pouring the blueberries or grapes into the fishbowl. Spoon the blue "water" over the fruit, arranging the gummy fish into the gelatin. Chill thoroughly. Let the kids fish for the snack with a ladle and be sure to restock the aquarium with extra candies. Makes 12 cups.

An Edible Fishbowl

Fluttery Creations

Young butterfly fans will flutter at the sight of sweet, gelatin butterflies. The idea came from *FamilyFun* contributor Jean Mitchel, who made them for her daughter's butterfly-themed birthday party.

- 2 3-ounce packages of cherry, blueberry, or lemon gelatin dessert
- 1 cup boiling water
   Twisted licorice
   Shoestring licorice
   Candy dots

In a medium-size bowl, dissolve the gelatin dessert with the boiling water. Pour the mixture into an 8-inch square pan and refrigerate for at least 3 hours. Using a 2½-inch butterfly cookie cutter (available at kitchen supply stores), carefully cut out the gelatin. Alternatively, cut a butterfly stencil out of waxed paper, place it on the gelatin, and cut around it with a sharp knife. If the butterflies are difficult to remove, dip the bottom of the pan in warm water for a few seconds.

Arrange a short length of twisted licorice in the center of the wings. For antennae, insert shoestring licorice into the heads. For added color, remove several candy dots from their paper and press them into the wings. Makes 9 butterflies.

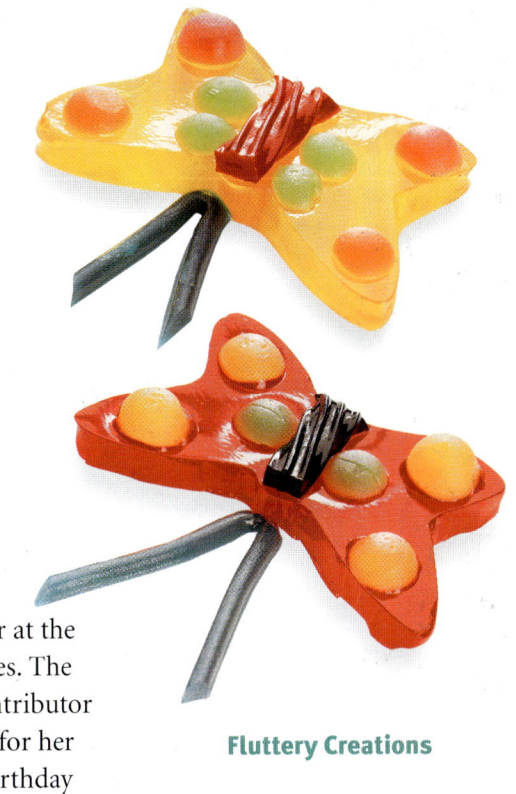

Fluttery Creations

No-Hands Jell-O Eating Contest

Every player is a winner in this birthday party or backyard carnival contest. Prepare several packages of flavored gelatin as directed. Then the judge should put 1 cup per contestant in a bowl and instruct each player to sit on his hands. When the kids hear "Go," they race to clean their bowls. The first clean plate wins, and the winner gets a full tummy.

After-School Snacks

Ice-Cream Flowerpots

Crackling Peanut Butter Balls

Our kid testers loved this messier, higher protein version of the Rice Krispies Treats classic.

- ¼ cup margarine
- 1 10-ounce package marshmallows
- ⅓ cup creamy peanut butter
- 6 cups crispy rice cereal

Melt margarine in a large saucepan over low heat. Add marshmallows and stir quickly until they are all melted (mini marshmallows melt faster). Turn off the burner and stir in peanut butter until mixed. Add the cereal and stir until coated. Butter your hands and roll the mixture into tennis ball shapes. Dry on waxed paper for 5 minutes before eating (store leftovers in plastic wrap). Makes 24 to 36 balls.

EDIBLE COLLAGES

Skip the paper and glue and let your kids use graham crackers and honey to create artwork they can eat. Fill a variety of small paper cups with goodies, such as raisins, chocolate or carob chips, carrot curls, gumdrops, gummy dinosaurs, or colored cereal. Spread a thin layer of honey (this is the glue for the collage) over the surface of a graham cracker. Using items from the cups, your kids can make any design in the honey — a rainbow, a funny face, a Matisse-like collage. When the collages are complete, the kids can dig in or save them for dessert.

Ice-Cream Flowerpots

With an ice-cream treat that looks like a flowerpot, you can invite your kids to go ahead and eat the daisies.

- 2 tablespoons chocolate cookie crumbs
- 1 scoop chocolate ice cream
  Green sprinkles
  Gumdrops
  Cookies or peanut butter cups
  Candy spearmint leaf

To make the "dirt," place 1 tablespoon of the chocolate crumbs into the bottom of a clear plastic cup. Add a scoop of softened chocolate ice cream, followed by a second layer of cookie crumbs. For grass, sow green sprinkles on the top. Place a straw (cut to a 6-inch length) into the center of the flowerpot and freeze. Meanwhile, make a flower by sticking gumdrops and cookies or peanut butter cups together with toothpicks. To serve, press the flower into the straw. Add a candy spearmint leaf. Makes 1 pot.

How To Make Ice Cream out of Snow

If you're lucky enough to be snowed in, scoop up a bowl of fresh snow and make a batch of ice cream. Place 1 pint whipping cream in a blender with ½ cup of sugar and your choice of flavoring: 1 teaspoon vanilla extract, ¼ cup chocolate syrup, 1 sliced banana, ¼ cup berries, or a few tablespoons of peanut butter. Blend on high for 3 minutes, or until the cream thickens. Meanwhile, fill a large mixing bowl with very clean snow. Pour the cream mixture over the snow, fold in crushed cookies, candies, or chocolate chips. Eat fast: it tastes best fresh. Serves 4 to 6.

Crunchy Snacks

Homemade Tortilla Chips

FamilyFun contributor Cynthia Caldwell's baked tortilla chips have been the hit of many family parties. Her advice: Don't toss leftover flour tortillas; turn them into chips.

- 2 8-inch flour tortillas
- 2 tablespoons olive oil
- Coarse salt

Preheat your broiler. Cut each tortilla into 8 wedges and lightly brush both sides with the oil. Arrange them on a jelly roll pan. Broil, flipping once when they begin to brown. When brown on both sides, remove and lightly sprinkle with salt. Serves 1.

Parmesan Chips:
Instead of salt, sprinkle with 1 to 2 teaspoons grated Parmesan cheese.

Garlic Chips:
Crush 1 clove of garlic and add to oil before brushing on tortillas.

Herb Tortillas:
Add 1 tablespoon chopped fresh herbs (parsley, cilantro, basil, or dill) to the oil, then brush on the tortillas.

Tortilla Chips

Nuke-able Nachos

The following makes enough for two to four kids, depending on their size and appetite. They will undoubtedly stretch and snap the gooey cheeses.

- 2 cups nacho chips
- 1 cup grated cheese (Monterey Jack, Cheddar, and/or Muenster)
- ½ cup diced tomatoes
- Leftover hamburger, refried beans, onions, jalapeño peppers, and olives (optional)
- Mild salsa and/or plain yogurt to taste

Place chips on a dinner plate. Sprinkle with the cheese, tomatoes, and the optional items if desired. Microwave on high for 1½ minutes. Serve with salsa and yogurt for dipping. Serves 2 to 3.

Potato Chip Nachos:
Substitute potato chips for tortilla chips.

TORTILLA TIP
To recrisp store-bought chips, microwave on high for 10 to 40 seconds.

Crunchy Teaser

Here's a Chinese stick puzzle you can solve and eat. Instead of using the traditional wooden sticks, try carrot sticks. Arrange eighteen into nine triangles as shown. The challenge: remove three sticks to change the pattern into six triangles. Like any good brainteaser, this puzzler has several solutions. How many can your family find?

FamilyFun COOKING

How To Flavor Popcorn

Plain and simple popcorn was served at the first Thanksgiving, and 300 years later, Americans are still enjoying this wholesome snack. Leave a bowl on the counter for when your kids come home from school — serve it as is or spice it up. To 4 cups of popped popcorn, add a flavoring:

Cheese Popcorn: Mix ¼ cup grated Parmesan cheese with 1½ tablespoons melted butter or margarine and toss with popcorn.

Sweet Cinnamon Popcorn: Shake popcorn with cinnamon sugar.

Zesty Popcorn: Top popcorn with grated Parmesan, then spice it up with a dash of garlic salt.

Tex-Mex Popcorn: Add a pinch of chili powder or taco seasoning to melted butter, pour over popcorn, and toss.

Pizza Popcorn: Mix a pinch of oregano, basil, and parsley into melted butter before tossing.

Power Popcorn: Sprinkle with 1 tablespoon of nutritional yeast for a healthy alternative to salt and butter.

Red-Hot Popcorn: Add a dash or more of hot sauce to melted butter and toss with popcorn.

Corny Caramel: Heat caramel or butterscotch sauce, pour over popcorn, and stir until coated. Spread on waxed paper to dry or roll into balls.

Flavored Popcorn

Witch's Brew

This party mix comes from five-year-old Jacob Mulhern of Cottage Grove, Wisconsin. The secret is a cupboard-clearing frenzy just prior to stirring. Anything goes in this recipe.

- 1 cup popped popcorn
- ¾ cup mini pretzels
- ½ cup each of mini marshmallows, chocolate chips, raisins, and Goldfish crackers

Stir all the ingredients together in a large bowl. Makes 3¾ cups.

Popcorn Art

Carry on the Native American tradition of making ornaments from popcorn. With a needle and thread, string popcorn and dried fruits (raisins, cherries, or cranberries) into bracelets and necklaces.

After-School Snacks

Meats

Back-to-Basics London Broil with Dijon-Herb Butter

Back-to-Basics London Broil

Dress up the all-American steak with one of our accompanying sauces. For a true back-to-basics dinner, support your town butcher — you'll often get the best cut of beef while contributing to an important local trade.

    2 pounds London broil or flank steak, 1 inch thick
        Coarse salt and black pepper
        Vegetable oil

Preheat your broiler or prepare the coals for grilling. Oil the broiling pan or grill before laying on the steaks. Rub the meat with the coarse salt and a bit of pepper. Cook 3 inches from the flame for 4 to 6 minutes per side for medium. To serve, slice the meat on the diagonal, following the grain. Serves 4 to 6.

Dijon-Herb Butter:
In a food processor or by hand, mix 6 tablespoons butter with 2 tablespoons mustard and 1 minced shallot. Add 8 chopped sprigs of parsley and 8 chopped chives. Pat into a log on waxed paper, refrigerate, and slice into rounds. Dot on warm steak.

Lemon Pepper:
Before you cook the steak, coat both sides with store-bought lemon pepper.

Veggie Smother:
Sauté 8 ounces of sliced mushrooms, 1 medium chopped onion, 1 sliced green pepper, and 1 crushed garlic clove in 1 tablespoon of butter or olive oil. Spoon over the warm steak just before serving.

Parsley Pesto:
In a food processor, blend 2 cups fresh parsley, 1 crushed garlic clove, and 2 tablespoons sunflower seeds with ⅓ cup olive oil. Add 3 tablespoons Parmesan cheese and ½ teaspoon salt. Dot on warm steak.

Horseradish Dipping Sauce:
Mix ½ cup sour cream with ¼ cup prepared horseradish and a dash of Worcestershire sauce.

Last-Minute Marinade:
Marinate the steak in any Italian salad dressing for at least 1 hour prior to cooking.

Perfect Burgers Every Time

Start with a ¾-inch-thick patty. Don't pack the meat too hard (you want to leave some air) or handle it too much. For a more flavorful burger, mix 1 pound ground beef with 4 drops Worcestershire sauce, 1 teaspoon crushed oregano, and salt and pepper, then form into patties. Grill the burgers, turning once (for well done, 10 minutes; for medium, 8 minutes.)

Dinner's Ready

MEXICAN FIESTA

Surprise your next dinner guests with a Mexican Fiesta. Set out the following and invite your guests to build their own Mexican creations.

Terrific Taco Filling (at right)

Shredded chicken

Refried beans

Mexican Rice (page 38)

Salsa

Tomatillo Salsa (at right)

Guacamole

Grated cheese

Chopped tomatoes

Sour cream

Diced red and green peppers

Minced jalapeños

Sliced black olives

Shredded lettuce

Diced red onions

Taco shells

Tortilla chips

Flour tortillas

Smiling Tostadas

Terrific Taco Filling

You can buy a package of taco shells or make your own by laying corn tortillas on the rack in an oven preheated to 300°. When they have softened, fold them over the oven rack grills so that they hang down, then heat until crisp, about 5 minutes.

- ½ tablespoon vegetable oil
- ½ cup chopped onion
- 1 pound lean ground beef
- 2 crushed garlic cloves
- ⅓ cup tomato juice, beef stock, water, or wine
- 2 tablespoons chili powder
- ½ teaspoon cumin
- Salt and pepper to taste

Heat the oil in a skillet over medium heat. Add the onion and sauté until translucent. Break up the ground beef with a fork and add it to the skillet. Stir in the garlic and continue stirring until the meat browns; drain out any excess fat. Stir in the tomato juice, chili powder, cumin, and salt and pepper. Continue cooking, stirring occasionally, until the mixture is heated through and the tastes are well combined. Spoon the beef mixture into prepared taco shells and top with your favorite accompaniments: shredded lettuce, olives, avocado, tomatoes, cheese. Makes 2½ to 3 cups.

Chicken Taco Filling:

For a leaner version, substitute ground chicken for the ground beef.

Turkey Taco Filling:

Substitute ground turkey for the beef.

28   FamilyFun COOKING

Beef Fajitas

This help-yourself meal, a Texas original, combines sizzling steak, onions, and peppers in a warm tortilla. Using skirt steak is traditional, but if you can't get this from your butcher, substitute flank steak.

- 1 tablespoon vegetable oil
- 2 pounds skirt steak or flank steak
- 4 small onions
- 2 red, green, or yellow peppers
- 8 to 10 flour tortillas
  Salsa
  Tomatillo Salsa (see recipe below)
  Guacamole

Heat the oil in a large nonstick frying pan over medium-high heat. Cook the steak on both sides, about 12 minutes for medium, and remove from the pan. Slice the onions and peppers and sauté until soft. Warm your tortillas in a skillet. Thinly slice the steak on the diagonal and arrange on a platter with the vegetables. Serve with salsas, guacamole, and the tortillas. Serves 4 to 6.

Grilled Fajitas:
Peel the onions and cut them in half; slice the peppers in half, too. Rub the vegetables with olive oil and place on your grill. Cook for several minutes, then push them aside. Cook the steak on both sides. Warm the tortillas on the grill. Slice the grilled vegetables and steak and serve with the tortillas.

Chicken Fajitas:
Substitute 2 boneless, skinless chicken breasts for the skirt steak.

Veggie Fajitas:
Substitute mixed vegetables — peppers, onions, carrots, zucchini, and squash — for the skirt steak.

Tomatillo Salsa

Tomatillos, also known as Mexican tomatoes, have a wonderful, mild lemon flavor and make an excellent sauce for any Mexican dish. Husk and rinse 1 pound of fresh tomatillos. In a large saucepan over medium heat, combine the tomatillos, 1 small jalapeño, seeded, veined, and chopped, 1 cup chopped onion, 1 cup water, and 3 to 4 crushed garlic cloves. Bring to a boil, reduce the heat to low, and simmer, covered, for about 15 minutes. In a blender or food processor, puree the juice of 1 lime, ¼ cup Italian parsley, and ¼ cup fresh cilantro. Add the tomatillo mixture, one third at a time, and process until smooth. Cool in the refrigerator. Makes 3½ cups.

Dinner's Ready

How To Make Smiling Tostadas

☛ **These open-faced sandwiches begin with a crispy shell. You can either purchase the shells or briefly fry corn tortillas in 2 tablespoons of oil. Spread the shell with taco filling or refried beans and grated cheese, then arrange shredded lettuce for hair, olive slices for eyes, a carrot slice for a nose, and tomato pieces for lips.**

Mexican Fiesta

Poultry

FunFact
The world's largest chicken weighed over 23 pounds (the average is 5 pounds).

Veggie Roast Chicken

Plain and Simple Roast Chicken

On weeknights, dinner in my household is a rushed affair, so once a month, I try to roast a chicken and make an old-fashioned Sunday dinner. We bring out the cloth napkins and candles and eat slowly, enjoying each other's company. This crispy-skin recipe welcomes your embellishments.

- 1 4- to 5-pound roasting chicken
- Half a lemon
- 1 large onion, sliced
- 2 tablespoons olive oil
- 1 teaspoon thyme
- ½ teaspoon coarse salt
- ¼ teaspoon pepper

Preheat the oven to 400°. Remove the giblets, thoroughly rinse the chicken, and pat dry. Squeeze the juice from the lemon half over the chicken, then stuff the half into the cavity. Close the cavity with small skewers and tie the legs together with string. Make a bed of onion slices in the bottom of the pan and place the chicken, breast side up, on the onions. Drizzle with the olive oil, sprinkle with the thyme, salt, and pepper and bake for 1¼ to 1½ hours, basting frequently, until the juices from behind the leg run clear. Let rest 5 minutes, then carve. Serves 4 to 6.

Veggie Roast Chicken:
Surround the chicken with peeled carrots and pearl onions, unpeeled new potatoes, and whole mushrooms. Serve with the roasted vegetables on the side.

Orange-Ginger Chicken:
Arrange orange slices on the bird, sprinkle with minced fresh ginger, and pour ½ cup orange juice over the top.

Apple-Hazelnut Chicken:
Place cored apple halves and peeled pearl onions in the roasting pan. Arrange apple slices on the bird and dash with cinnamon. Drizzle apple brandy over the bird for a full flavor. Ten minutes before the chicken is done, add 1 cup hazelnuts to the pan.

Lemon-Rosemary Chicken:
Place lemon slices on the chicken and sprinkle generously with rosemary and a little olive oil.

Stuffed Chicken:
Just before roasting, loosely stuff the chicken with your favorite stuffing recipe. Increase the cooking time by 25 minutes.

FamilyFun COOKING

Potato Chip Chicken Fingers

Potato Chip Chicken Fingers

These irresistible fingers get their crunch not from deep-frying but from potato chips. Experiment with chip flavors, from barbecue to sour cream and chive.

- 1 whole boneless, skinless chicken breast
- 5 to 6 ounces potato chips, plain, barbecue, or sour cream
- 1 egg
- 2 tablespoons milk

Preheat the oven to 400°. Cut the chicken into finger-size pieces. Fill a large, sealable plastic bag with the potato chips, seal the bag, and crush the chips with the back of a wooden spoon.

In a small bowl, whisk the egg and milk. Dip the chicken pieces into the egg mixture, then into the bag. Shake gently to cover. Place on an ungreased cookie sheet. Bake for 20 minutes, flipping once during the cooking time. Serve with barbecue sauce, salsa, or honey mustard dip. Serves 4.

Bat Wings

Soy sauce and honey transform ordinary chicken wings into exotic bat wings — a special Halloween treat.

- ½ cup honey
- 1 cup soy sauce
- 1 cup water
- 2 crushed garlic cloves
- 2 dozen chicken wings

Combine the honey, soy sauce, water, and garlic in a large baking dish, reserving ⅔ cup in a bowl for the sauce. Toss in chicken wings and marinate for at least 1 hour. Broil for 10 minutes on each side, allowing the wings to char slightly. Present with sauce. Serves 8.

MOM'S RESTAURANT

FamilyFun reader Sue Jones, of Altamont, New York, created an "at home" restaurant that has her family jumping for leftovers. She dreamed it up because it didn't make sense for her to prepare a new meal when the refrigerator was already overcrowded. On the other hand, when the response to "What's for dinner?" was "Leftovers!" her family predictably groaned. So Sue inventoried her refrigerator and made a menu for Mom's Restaurant. (She used her computer to write the menu, but a handwritten one will suffice.)

At dinnertime, she met her family at the entrance to the dining room, apron on, menus in hand, and asked, "How many in your party?" The first response

was a giggle. Then they said, "Three." When Sue returned with a notepad, they were ready to place an order.

If your kids really take to this idea, you might suggest they occasionally play waiter and head chef themselves, deciding what kind of restaurant to have (fast food, ethnic, or gourmet), and what to make for an upcoming meal. If they add prices to their menu and you request an itemized bill, the kids will also have to do some quick math.

Dinner's Ready 31

Panfried Fish-in-a-Flash

Candlelight Dinners

One cold evening, the five-year-old son of *FamilyFun* reader Julie Dunlap found an old box of candles and insisted on setting several on the table. The golden flames cast a magic spell — the kids spoke in hushed voices, and everyone inched closer to the table as they told stories and fantasized about life in a frontier cabin. Now, the glow of candles and conversation often fills their house, and the warmth and closeness last long after the flames are blown out.

Fish-in-a-Flash Mix

This fish coating works well with almost any filet — scrod, sole, even trout. For extra crunch, use cornmeal instead of the flour.

- ½ cup all-purpose flour
- 2 teaspoons parsley
- 1 teaspoon dried minced onions
- 1 teaspoon garlic powder
- 1 teaspoon basil
- ½ teaspoon salt
- ¼ teaspoon dried lemon peel
- ¼ teaspoon pepper
- Pinch of cayenne pepper

Shake all the ingredients in a large, sealable plastic bag. Makes 1 cup.

Panfried Fish-in-a-Flash:

Gently shake two to three 8-ounce fish filets in the bag of Fish-in-a-Flash Mix. Heat 1 tablespoon butter in a heavy frying pan set on the stove over medium-high heat or on a grill 1 inch above the hot coals. Cook the filets for 6 minutes, flip, and continue cooking until the flesh flakes. Serves 4 to 6.

Citrus Swordfish

This flavorful marinade is ideal for any firm fish (swordfish, tuna, or hake).

- ¼ cup olive oil
- 4 crushed garlic cloves
- 2 teaspoons ground cumin
- ¼ cup chopped fresh Italian parsley or cilantro
- Juice from 2 lemons
- Salt and pepper to taste
- 1 to 2 pounds swordfish

In the bowl of a food processor, combine the oil, garlic, cumin, parsley, and lemon juice. Puree until smooth and add salt and pepper to taste. (You can also do this by hand with a whisk in a large mixing bowl.)

Place the fish in a shallow dish with the sauce and marinate for several hours or overnight. Toss occasionally. Preheat your broiler or prepare the coals for grilling. Broil or grill the fish 3 inches from the flames for 6 to 8 minutes, flip, and continue cooking until it flakes. Serves 4 to 6.

FamilyFun COOKING

Fish & Seafood

Salmon Steaks with Quick Dill Sauce

As the Japanese have known for years, fish is a light and healthy dinner option, worthy of being served at least once a week. Whether you're shopping at your local grocer's or a fish market, always look for the freshest fish. It should have a firm, moist flesh and a sweet smell — never a fishy smell, which is a sure sign of aging. Salmon is great with this sauce, but any fresh filet you choose will work.

Quick Dill Sauce:
- ½ cup sour cream
- ¼ cup mayonnaise
- 2 tablespoons milk
- 1½ teaspoons dill
- 1 small crushed garlic clove
- Salt and pepper

Fish:
- 4 6-ounce salmon steaks, 1 inch thick
- Half a lemon

In a small bowl, whisk the sour cream, mayonnaise, and milk until creamy. Add the dill, garlic, and salt and pepper to taste. Stir well; set aside.

Preheat your broiler or prepare the coals for grilling. Rinse the salmon steaks and pat them dry. Squeeze the lemon over the steaks and sprinkle with salt and pepper. Broil or grill the steaks 3 inches from the heat for 8 to 10 minutes, or until the meat has turned from a bright pink to a pale orange. Serves 4 to 6.

Fast Fish Filets

The microwave turns seafood into fast food that is nutritious and delicious.

- 2 to 3 fish filets, any white fish
- Salt and pepper
- Juice of half a lemon
- 1½ tablespoons chopped fresh herbs, such as dill, parsley, mint, cilantro, or sage
- 4 thin lemon slices
- Toppings (see right)

Rinse the filets and pat dry. Salt and pepper both sides and lay them like the spokes of a wheel in a glass pie pan with the thickest portions on the edges. Sprinkle with the lemon juice and herbs and top with the lemon slices. Cover and cook on high for 3 to 6 minutes, or until the fish flakes. Add toppings. Serves 4.

Salmon Steak with Quick Dill Sauce

Fish Filets and...
- **Tartar Sauce:** Mix ½ cup mayonnaise with 2 to 3 tablespoons relish.
- **Quick Cocktail Sauce:** Mix ½ cup catsup with 2 tablespoons horseradish.
- **Salsa**
- **Quick Dill Sauce:** See recipe at left.
- **Teriyaki sauce:** Buy at your grocer's.

Dinner's Ready

Pasta

Down-home Spaghetti

On Top of Spaghetti

For pasta pronto, top your noodles with one of these savory combos.

☛ Stir-fried vegetables with garlic and herbs

☛ Tuna, capers, and a little cream

☛ Fresh tomatoes, olive oil, red wine vinegar, basil, and Mozzarella cheese

☛ Italian salad dressing

☛ Chopped scallions, peas or broccoli, olive oil, and lemon zest

☛ Can of stewed tomatoes, chopped olives, oregano, and black pepper

☛ Can of chopped clams sautéed with butter and garlic

☛ Strips of chicken breast sautéed in olive oil with black pepper and parsley

☛ Soy sauce and ginger

☛ Salsa and red or black beans

Down-home Spaghetti Sauce

There are a number of good sauces on the market, but if you have the time, it is easy, gratifying, and less expensive to make your own. This recipe requires a long, slow simmer, but little chopping and stirring. It is adaptable (you can add chopped peppers or other vegetables), but if your kids are the kind who search for and toss out any add-ins, the sauce is equally good without the extras.

- 2 tablespoons olive oil
- 1 cup chopped onion
- 2 ribs celery, thinly sliced
- 1 to 2 carrots, chopped
- 1 pound ground beef, ground turkey, or ground sweet Italian sausage, or a mixture (optional)
- ⅓ cup white or red wine
- 2 28-ounce cans Italian plum tomatoes, whole or crushed
- 1 teaspoon oregano
- 1 teaspoon basil
  Salt and pepper to taste

In a large skillet or pot, sauté the olive oil and onion over medium heat until the onion is soft. Add the celery and carrots and cook 8 to 10 minutes (lower the heat, if necessary, to prevent the vegetables from browning). For a meat sauce, crumble the ground meat into the pan; cook, stirring, until the meat loses its pink color.

Turn the heat to high, add the wine, and cook, stirring, until the wine evaporates. Add the tomatoes and their juice (if you are using whole tomatoes, break them up in the pan). When the mixture begins to bubble, reduce the heat to low and simmer for 1½ hours, stirring occasionally. Finally, mix in the oregano, basil, and salt and pepper, and remove from the heat. Serve immediately, save for 1 to 2 days in the refrigerator, or cool, then freeze. Makes 2½ quarts.

Lasagna a la Mom

If you're tight on time, make this dish with uncooked noodles (add an extra cup of sauce to the bottom of the pan). No one will ever know the difference.

- 2 cups low-fat ricotta cheese
- ½ cup grated Parmesan cheese
- 1 egg, lightly beaten
- ¼ cup chopped fresh parsley
- Salt and pepper to taste
- Dash of nutmeg
- 2 tablespoons butter
- 2½ cups spaghetti sauce (see Down-home Spaghetti Sauce, at left)
- ½ pound lasagna noodles, cooked according to package directions
- ½ pound Mozzarella, grated

Mix the ricotta and Parmesan cheeses, egg, and parsley. Add the salt, pepper, and nutmeg. Butter a 13- by 9- by 2-inch baking pan and dot sparingly with a bit of the tomato sauce. Place a layer of noodles over the bottom of the pan, overlapping as little as possible. Spread half of the ricotta mixture over the noodles, then the tomato sauce, then the Mozzarella. Repeat layering, finishing with a layer of noodles, the remaining sauce, and a sprinkle of Parmesan. At this point the lasagna may be refrigerated, frozen, or baked. Bake in a preheated 375° oven for 20 minutes, or until hot and bubbling. Remove from the oven and settle for 10 minutes before slicing. Serves 6.

Spinach Lasagna:

Defrost and drain a 10-ounce package of frozen spinach and spread it over the ricotta layers.

Turkey Sausage Lasagna:

Cook ½ pound ground turkey sausage and layer it on top of each of the ricotta layers.

Spaghetti Carbonara

The smell of bacon frying in the pan is enough to heighten any kids' curiosity about this Italian carbonara.

- 1 pound dried spaghetti
- 1 pound bacon, cut in 1-inch pieces
- ½ cup chopped onion
- 2 eggs, lightly beaten
- ½ cup grated Parmesan or Romano cheese
- Salt and pepper to taste
- 2 tablespoons heavy cream

Prepare the spaghetti according to package directions. While the pasta is cooking, sauté the bacon in a large skillet until crisp. Drain on paper towels and reserve 3 teaspoons of fat from the pan. Add the onion and sauté until soft; set aside.

Drain the cooked pasta and return it to the pot over very low heat. Toss in the bacon fat and bacon, onion, eggs, cheese, salt, pepper, and cream. Cook until all the ingredients are well blended and heated through. Serves 4 to 6.

Slurping Spaghetti

How can your kids avoid getting tomato sauce everywhere when they eat spaghetti? According to Ms. Demeanor, the trick is to twirl just three or four strands with your fork, which should spin into the perfect mouthful. You can put a spoon underneath the fork to get the spaghetti under control. The goal is to pick up any loose ends before you bring the pasta up to your mouth.

Lasagna a la Mom

Dinner's Ready 35

Carrot Coins

PLANTING CARROTS FOR SNOWMEN

The Shilling family of Fayetteville, West Virginia, started an annual tradition by accident. The first year their son planted carrots, they never got around to harvesting them all. After the first snowman of the season was built, a dash to the refrigerator brought a moan: "No carrots for the nose, Mom." Then mom, Terri, remembered the ones left in the ground, and sure enough, she dug down through the snow and frozen ground and pulled up beautiful carrots. Now, every spring the Shillings plant a special area of carrots to be saved for snowmen's noses.

Carrot Coins

Cynthia Caldwell, a regular *FamilyFun* contributor, learned to make these when she was a Girl Scout. She has passed her love of carrot coins on to her daughter, Isabelle.

- 3 to 4 carrots
- ½ cup water
- 2 tablespoons brown sugar
- 1 tablespoon butter
- 1 teaspoon cider vinegar
- Salt and pepper to taste

Peel and slice the carrots into thin rounds or coins. Place them in a medium-size frying pan with the water. Cover and cook over medium-high heat for 6 to 7 minutes, or until the water has nearly evaporated and the carrots are soft. Uncover and add the sugar, butter, and cider vinegar. Turn up the heat and sauté, stirring for 2 to 3 minutes. A copper-colored glaze will form over the carrots. Season with salt and pepper and serve. Serves 3 to 5.

Flower Power Carrots:

For a special occasion, cut slightly wider carrots into coins. Using an aspic cutter (tiny cookie cutter), cut each coin into a flower.

Oven-Roasted String Beans

When it's too cold to grill, I roast my vegetables for a great smoky flavor.

- 2 pounds green and/or yellow string beans, washed and trimmed
- 1 tablespoon olive oil
- Salt

Toss the beans with oil and spread them out on a cookie sheet. Sprinkle with salt. Roast in a 450° preheated oven for 10 minutes. Serves 8.

Oven-Roasted Asparagus:

Substitute 2 pounds asparagus for the beans and roast for 8 minutes. Serves 8.

Broccoli Trees

Watch the vegetables disappear as your kids create and eat a forest of broccoli. Prepare a dip by combining ¼ cup light sour cream, ⅓ cup mayonnaise, ½ teaspoon sugar, 1 tablespoon lemon juice, and 1 tablespoon chopped fresh basil leaves. To make the trees, cut 3 cups broccoli florets and peel 4 carrots. Cut each carrot widthwise and then lengthwise into 4 pieces. Assemble on a plate by laying 3 carrot pieces for a trunk with the broccoli florets as the leaves. Spread dip under the trunks for the forest floor. Makes 5 trees.

FamilyFun COOKING

Vegetables

Asparagus with Sesame-Orange Dipping Sauce

Although asparagus is available from January to June, the biggest, freshest supply hits the markets in early spring (March and April). This dish can be served warm or cold, depending on your family's preference.

- 1 pound asparagus, trimmed
- ½ teaspoon salt

Sauce:
- 2 tablespoons orange juice
- 1 teaspoon orange rind, finely grated
- ¼ cup olive oil
- 1 teaspoon sesame oil
- Sea salt to taste
- Freshly ground pepper to taste

Find a saucepan wide enough to hold the asparagus spears lengthwise and set it over medium-high heat. Fill about three quarters with water, add the salt, and bring to a boil. Plunge the spears into the boiling water, return to a boil, and cook until the spears are just tender when pierced with a fork, about 2 to 6 minutes depending on thickness (do not overcook). Rinse under cold running water to stop cooking and then drain on a clean kitchen towel.

To prepare the sauce, whisk together the orange juice, orange rind, olive oil, sesame oil, and coarse salt and pepper until they are well blended. Arrange the asparagus on a large serving platter with dipping sauce on the side. Serves 4.

Asparagus with Sesame-Orange Dipping Sauce

Sesame Broccoli

When cooked in the microwave oven, broccoli keeps its bright green color and crispiness. For even more crunch, I add sesame seeds.

- 2 tablespoons sesame seeds
- 1 head broccoli, cut into florets with the tough stems removed
- 2 tablespoons water
- Salt and pepper to taste

Spread the sesame seeds on a paper towel. Microwave on high for 3 to 4 minutes, or until the seeds turn light brown. Set aside. Place the broccoli in a microwave-safe casserole with the stems pointing out. Add the water, cover tightly, and cook on high for about 4 minutes. Uncover and let stand for 2 minutes before draining and tossing with the sesame seeds and seasoning. Serves 4.

Veggie Toppers

Give your vegetables extra flavor with a sprinkle of the following:

- ☛ Toasted chopped nuts, such as almonds, walnuts, and peanuts
- ☛ Crumbled bacon
- ☛ Toasted sesame seeds
- ☛ Bread crumbs
- ☛ Chopped fresh herbs
- ☛ Grated Parmesan or Cheddar cheese
- ☛ Chopped hard-boiled egg

Side Dishes & Salads

Rices & Grains

Couscous with Peas

Couscous with Peas

Originating in North Africa, this fine, grainlike cereal cooks even faster than rice or potatoes. You can serve it plain, embellish it with peas and onion as it is here, or experiment with just about any fresh herb or chopped vegetable.

- 1 onion, diced
- 1 crushed garlic clove
- 1 tablespoon olive oil
- 1 cup frozen peas
- 1 tablespoon minced fresh dill
  Salt and pepper to taste
- 1½ cups vegetable or chicken stock
- 1 cup couscous

Sauté the onion and garlic in the oil in a saucepan over medium heat until translucent, about 5 minutes. Stir in the peas, dill, salt, pepper, and stock and bring to a boil. Add the couscous, cover, and return to a boil. Remove from the heat and let the mixture sit for 5 minutes, or until the liquid is absorbed. This can sit, covered, for about 10 more minutes or may be served immediately. Fluff with a fork before serving. Serves 4.

White Long-Grain Rice

White Short-Grain Rice

Brown Rice

Wild Rice

How To Cook Rice

Cooked just right, plain rice makes a wonderful, healthy side dish. Enhance the flavor by using broth or sprinkling it with herbs and spices. Directions are for 3 to 4 cups cooked rice.

Long-Grain: Boil 2 cups water, add 1 cup rice, stir, cover, and simmer for 15 to 20 minutes.

Short-Grain: Boil 1½ cups water, add 1 cup rice, stir, cover, and simmer for 15 to 20 minutes.

Brown Rice: Boil 2½ cups water, add 1 cup rice, stir, cover, and simmer for 30 minutes.

Wild Rice: Boil 4 cups water, add 1 cup rice, stir, cover, and simmer for 35 to 40 minutes.

FunFact
Fifty percent of all the world's rice is eaten within 8 miles of where it is grown.

FamilyFun COOKING

Mexican Rice

A meal wouldn't be Mexican without a side of rice and beans, whether inside or alongside a tortilla. This seasoned rice is flavored with everything Mexican — cumin, jalapeño, garlic, and more. To save time preparing it, use a food processor to chop the onion, garlic, and pepper.

- 1 tablespoon vegetable oil
- 1½ cups white rice
- 1 16-ounce can Italian plum tomatoes, peeled and chopped, with their juice
- 2 onions, chopped
- 2 crushed garlic cloves
- 1 jalapeño pepper, seeded, veined, and chopped
- ½ teaspoon cumin
- 2 cups chicken stock, tomato juice, or water
- 1 cup frozen corn kernels (optional)
- 1 cup frozen peas (optional)
- ½ cup chopped fresh or frozen carrots (optional)
- Fresh parsley or cilantro (optional)

Heat the oil in a large saucepan and add the rice. Stir for about 3 minutes. Add the tomatoes, onion, garlic, pepper, cumin, and the stock, tomato juice, or water, as well as a combination or all of the corn, peas, and carrots.

Bring to a boil and simmer, covered, until the liquid is absorbed and the rice is tender, about 15 minutes. Garnish with chopped fresh parsley or cilantro. Serves 6 to 8.

Seasoned Rice Mix

Seasoned Rice Mixes

FamilyFun contributor Susan Purdy says these quick rice mixes make wonderful gifts from the kitchen. Store in widemouthed jars or take-out cartons.

Herb Rice:
- 1 cup uncooked long-grain white rice
- 2 beef or vegetable bouillon cubes
- 1 teaspoon green onion flakes
- ½ teaspoon each: rosemary, marjoram or oregano, and thyme leaves
- ½ teaspoon salt or celery salt

Curried Rice:
- 1 cup uncooked long-grain white rice
- 2 chicken or vegetable bouillon cubes
- ½ to 1 teaspoon curry powder
- 1 teaspoon dried minced onion
- ½ teaspoon ground cumin
- ½ teaspoon parsley flakes
- ½ teaspoon salt or celery salt

In a large mixing bowl, stir all the ingredients for either rice and pour into a sealable container.

Seasoned Rice:

In a large saucepan combine either the Herb or Curried Rice mixture with 2 cups cold water. Bring to a boil. Reduce the heat to low, stir once, and cover. Simmer for 14 to 20 minutes, or until the liquid is absorbed. Serves 4.

Kids Dig Rice

At nursery school, the favorite activity of *FamilyFun* reader Janet Buckley's four-year-old son is playing at the rice table, so she decided to create one for home use. After sealing the cracks of a large cardboard box with colorful hockey tape and decorating it with stickers, they filled the box with ten pounds of uncooked, inexpensive rice and added small pasta (orzo and tubettini), which they had painted with watercolors. With spoons, cups, and scoops, Sean pours and measures the rice, hides things in it, and builds hills and valleys.

Potatoes

Potato Pals

If your kids are wandering around the kitchen antsy for dinner, let them dress up a crowd of potato people. Begin with a plain potato and slice off the bottom. Using toothpicks or pushpins, attach cutout paper eyes, noses, mouths, or clothing. Other kitchen items — raisins, pasta, straws, peanuts, and muffin cup liners — can become ears, buttons, hair, or hats. After dinner, host a potato fashion show.

Red Potatoes with Garlic and Rosemary

The garlic in this side dish is cooked in its skin, so that it comes out sweet and creamy. To eat, just hold a clove by its "tail" and pull out the insides.

- 2 pounds of small, new red potatoes, scrubbed and halved
- 10 cloves of garlic, left in their skins, excess paper removed
-   Sea salt to taste
-   Black pepper to taste
- 1 tablespoon chopped fresh rosemary or 1 teaspoon dried

Preheat the oven to 350°. Lightly oil a large roasting pan or baking dish and arrange the potatoes and garlic in one layer. Sprinkle with the salt, pepper, and rosemary. Cover tightly with foil and bake for 1 hour, or until the potatoes are soft when poked with a fork. Serves about 6.

Classic Mashed Potatoes

Hand-mashed and flavored to perfection, homemade mashed potatoes are my favorite comfort food. They may seem like a lot of work, but a little peeling and mashing are certainly worth the effort. Serve them as they are or embellish them with toppings.

- 4 to 5 large potatoes, peeled
- ½ to 1 cup milk
- 2 tablespoons butter
-   Salt and pepper to taste
-   Pinch of nutmeg (optional)

Cover the potatoes with cold water and bring to a boil. Cook for 20 minutes, or until tender. (Be careful to watch the pot; potatoes have a tendency to boil over.)

While the spuds are cooking, slowly heat the milk and butter. When the potatoes are done, drain them and add half the hot milk mixture. Mash the potatoes with a handheld potato masher or an electric mixer. Keep adding the hot milk until you reach the proper consistency (which, of course, varies from family to family). Season with salt, pepper, and nutmeg, if desired. Serves 4 to 6.

Spuds with Jewels:

In a frying pan, heat 1 teaspoon of vegetable oil and briefly sauté 1 diced red pepper (add hot peppers such as green jalapeño for fire). Stir in ½ teaspoon basil. Immediately pour on top of mashed potatoes.

Green Potatoes:

Use an electric mixer to blend 1 to 2 cups chopped cooked spinach into mashed potatoes until they turn green.

Red Potatoes with Garlic and Rosemary

Red Coats:
Use purple, red, or new potatoes with their skins on.

The Cheddar Broccoli:
Mix grated Cheddar cheese with 1 cup chopped, steamed broccoli florets and fold into the mashed spuds.

Prague Potatoes:
Panfry 4 strips of bacon until crisp. Remove from the pan and add 1 diced onion, cooking until translucent. Crumble the bacon into the onion. Top mashed potatoes with bacon, onion, and drippings, using about 1½ teaspoons or less of fat per serving.

Golden Broil:
Spread prepared mashed potatoes in an oven-to-table baking dish. Drizzle ½ cup heavy cream over the top and sprinkle with Parmesan cheese. Broil until the top turns golden.

Breakfast for Dinner:
Serve mashed potatoes in a large bowl topped with 3 to 4 chopped hard-boiled eggs and chopped fresh parsley and chives.

Tatties 'n' Neeps:
For the Scots' way of using up leftover mashed potatoes, mix equal amounts of mashed potatoes and mashed turnips.

Colcannon:
Mix mashed potatoes with 1½ cups shredded, cooked, and drained cabbage or kale.

Bangers and Mash:
Try this English recipe: serve plain mashed potatoes with broiled or pan-seared sausages ("bangers") on the side.

Fenced-in Spuds:
Surround a mound of mashed potatoes with a "fence" of steamed green beans and carrot sticks.

Toppings for Mashed Spuds:
- Chopped black olives and scallions
- Sautéed mushrooms
- Crosscut leeks cooked in butter until soft
- Herbed bread crumbs
- Toasted sesame seeds
- Salsa
- Cheddar or Parmesan cheese
- Crumbled cooked bacon
- Sautéed onion with red or green peppers
- Chopped basil and fresh tomatoes
- Cumin and/or chili powder

Red Coats

The Cheddar Broccoli

Prague Potatoes

Green Potatoes

Spuds with Jewels

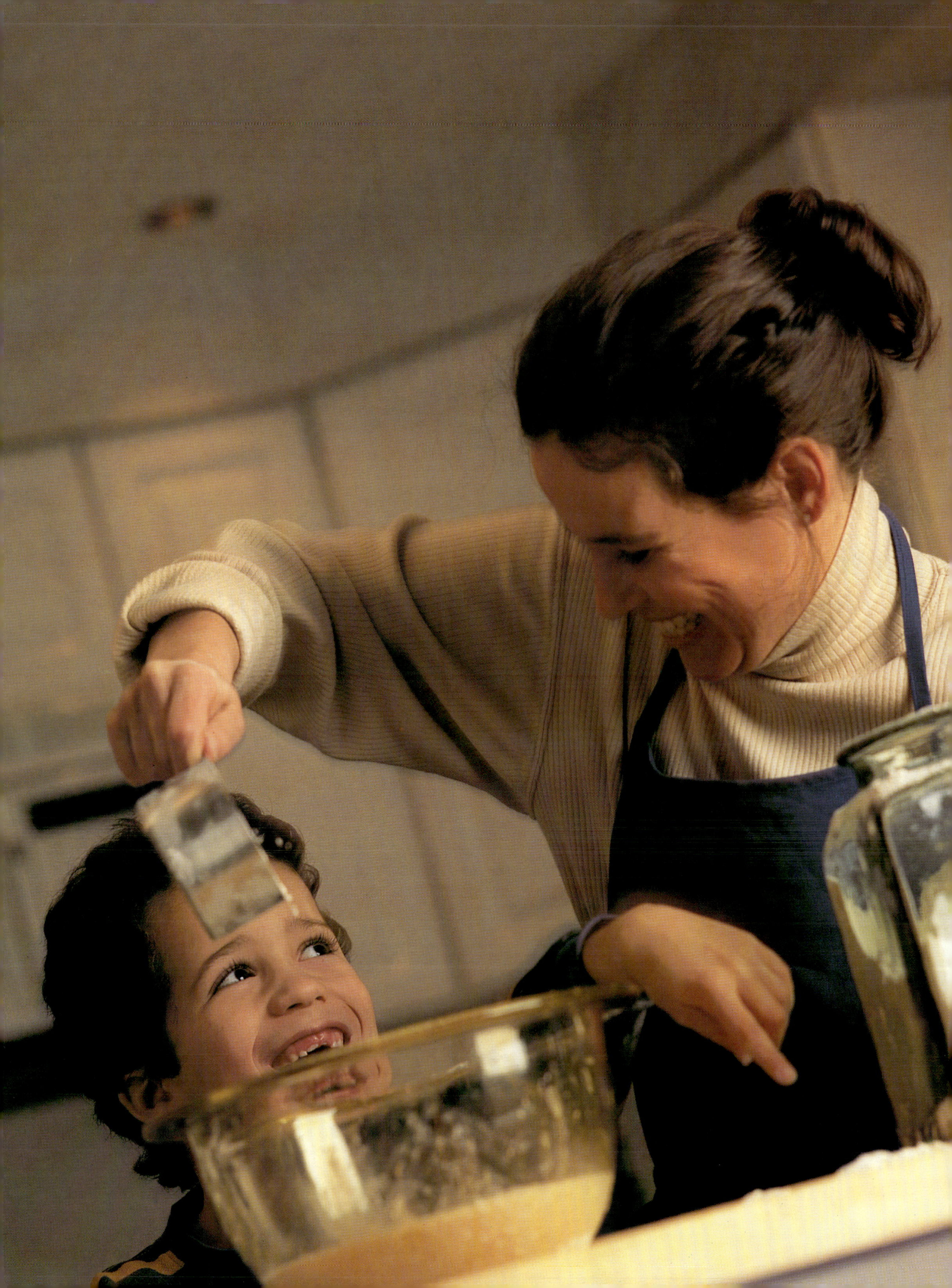

Cookies

Giant Chocolate Chip Cookies

When Ruth Wakefield added chopped chocolate to her basic butter cookie recipe at the Toll House Inn, chocolate chip became the most popular cookie in America. Here, we've updated Ruth's 1930s recipe to a '90s extravaganza. The goodies that go in them are up to you (chocolate chips, crushed toffee bars, butterscotch chips, or M&M's). The size they take is your decision, too — you can make them as small as a dime or as big as your hands.

- 2¼ cups all-purpose flour
- ¾ teaspoon baking powder
- ½ teaspoon salt
- 1 cup unsalted butter, softened
- ¾ cup sugar
- ½ cup packed light brown sugar
- 2 eggs
- 2 teaspoons vanilla extract
- 2 cups semisweet chocolate chips

In a large bowl, mix the flour, baking powder, and salt. In a separate bowl, cream the butter and sugars, then add the eggs, one at a time, mixing well after each addition. Stir in the vanilla extract, then gradually stir in the flour mixture until combined. Add the chips and stir again. For chewy cookies, refrigerate the dough for 2 hours or overnight.

Preheat the oven to 300°. Using a ⅓-cup measuring cup, drop the dough onto a baking sheet, leaving 3 inches between mounds. Bake for 30 to 35 minutes, or until light brown. Cool for 5 minutes, then transfer to a wire rack and cool completely. Makes 15 giant cookies.

Monster M&M's:
Substitute M&M's for the 2 cups of chocolate chips.

Monster Chip & Nut:
Stir in 1 cup chopped walnuts, pecans, or other nuts with the chips.

Monster Pops:
Before baking the cookies, insert a Popsicle stick into the dough.

Monster Stir-ins:
Try other chips, such as peanut butter, butterscotch, or white chocolate.

Mini Cookies:
Use mini chips or M&M's. Measure out rounded teaspoons of dough, leaving 1½ inches between cookies. Bake for 17 to 20 minutes. Makes 85.

Can I Have Dessert?

Cookie Decorating

You don't need a lot of expensive equipment to create edible works of art— most of the stuff is already in your kitchen.

- Cookie cutters
- Aspic cutters (tiny cookie cutters)
- Garlic press for squeezing dough to make hair, manes, and swirls (don't pile it on too thick or it won't cook all the way through)
- Kitchen utensils and clean toys to make patterns in the dough
- Tubes of decorator's icing and/or assorted colors of homemade frosting in pastry bags for icing the cookies
- Colored sprinkles, M&M's, jelly beans, gumdrops, red hots, licorice, chocolate chips, or raisins for decorating the cookies

Sugar Cookies

This foolproof recipe will unleash the cookie monster in anyone. Creative cooks can cut the dough with any size cookie cutter, color it red, white, and blue, flavor it with chocolate, almond, and lemon, or use the baked cookies as an empty canvas for a frosting design.

- 1 cup butter, softened
- ¾ cup sugar
- 1 large egg
- 1 teaspoon vanilla extract
- 2¾ cups all-purpose flour
- 1 teaspoon baking soda
- 1 teaspoon cream of tartar

In a large bowl, cream the butter and sugar until fluffy. Add the egg and beat well, then mix in the vanilla extract. In a separate bowl, combine the flour, baking soda, and cream of tartar. Add the flour mixture to the butter mixture, one third at a time, until thoroughly combined.

Divide the dough into two equal portions and flatten each into a disk. Cover each disk in plastic wrap and refrigerate for 2 to 3 hours, or until the dough is firm enough to work with. If it becomes too firm, soften at room temperature for about 5 minutes.

Preheat the oven to 350°. On a lightly floured board, roll out the dough until it is about ¼ inch thick. Cut out cookies with cutters or by hand.

Using a metal spatula, carefully transfer the cookies to a baking sheet, leaving about 2 inches between them. Bake for 8 to 10 minutes, or until lightly browned around the edges.

Remove the cookie sheet from the oven, place it on a wire rack, and cool for 2 to 3 minutes. Using a metal spatula, transfer the cookies to the rack and cool completely. Repeat this procedure with the remaining chilled dough. Form any extra dough scraps into a disk, chill if necessary before rerolling, then continue until all the dough has been used. Baked cookies can be stored in an airtight container in the freezer for up to 1 month before frosting and decorating and for up to 3 days at room temperature. Makes about 3 dozen cookies, depending on their size.

Pinwheel cookies

Colored Sugar Cookies:

To make colored sugar cookies, mix and knead liquid or paste food coloring, drop by drop, into the basic sugar cookie dough until it reaches the desired hue.

Chocolate Cookie Dough:

After the last third of flour has been incorporated in the dough, mix in 2 ounces of melted and slightly cooled unsweetened chocolate.

Almond Cookie Dough:

Stir 1 teaspoon of almond extract into the dough right after the last third of flour has been incorporated.

Lemon Cookie Dough:

After the last third of flour has been added to the dough, stir in 2 teaspoons of grated lemon peel.

Appliquéd Stars

Cookie Necklace

Appliquéd Stars:

For this multicolored cookie, you'll need three different dough colors and two or three similarly shaped cutters in differing sizes. Cut a large star (or another shape) out of one color of cookie dough and place it on a baking sheet. Using a smaller star cutter, cut out the center of the first star and remove it. Use the smaller cutter to cut out a star from a contrasting color and insert it into the center of the big star. Repeat with a third color of dough and the smallest cutter, if desired. Gently pinch the seams between the doughs so they won't separate during baking. Bake for 10 to 12 minutes.

Pinwheel Cookies:

Roll out chocolate and sugar doughs separately between sheets of plastic wrap into 12- by 8-inch rectangles. Remove the top sheet of wrap from one dough rectangle. Remove both sheets from the second rectangle and place that dough on top of the first. Starting with one of the 12-inch sides, roll up the doughs, jelly roll fashion. (Do not roll the plastic wrap up in between the dough, but wrap it around the outside of the roll.) Refrigerate or freeze for 1 hour, or until firm. Remove the plastic wrap, cut the roll into ¼-inch-thick slices, and place them on baking sheets. Bake for 10 minutes, or until the cookies are just lightly browned.

Cookie Necklaces:

Use letter-shaped cutters or cardboard templates to create names and words from the dough. Punch a hole in the top of each letter with a drinking straw. After baking the cookies for 10 minutes, cool and decorate. String them together on a piece of thin licorice.

Alphabet Cookies:

These edible letters can be used as spelling aids, word game pieces, or treats. Roll the dough into three cylinders (about 1 inch in diameter), cover, and refrigerate for 1 hour. Slice the logs into ¼-inch-thick rounds. Bake for about 10 minutes. When cool, use icing to inscribe a letter on each one. The most commonly used letters in the English language are *A, E, I, S,* and *T,* so make extras of these. The least commonly used are *Q, X,* and *Z,* so one of each should suffice.

Easier Cookie Baking

☛ Cut from the edge of the dough to the center, removing the cookies as you go.
☛ Position the oven rack in the center of the oven. If you use two racks, switch the positions of the baking sheets halfway through baking.
☛ Bake similar-size cookies together on one baking sheet so they are done at the same time.
☛ Don't run your hot baking sheets under cold water — the abrupt temperature change can cause them to warp.

Alphabet Cookies

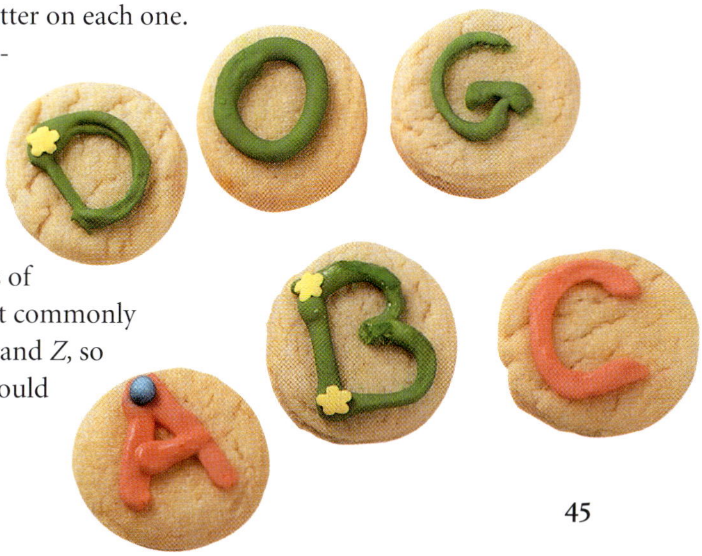

Can I Have Dessert?

Cakes

Chocolate Celebration Cake

Cubcakes

Chocolate Celebration Cake

When frosted with chocolate icing, this cake is a celebration of the richest chocolate flavor around.

    5   ounces unsweetened chocolate,
         coarsely chopped
    2   cups all-purpose flour
    2½   teaspoons baking powder
    ¼   teaspoon salt
    ¾   cup unsalted butter, softened
    1½   cups sugar
    2   teaspoons vanilla extract
    3   large eggs, at room temperature
    1¼   cups milk

Preheat the oven to 350°. Lightly butter two 9-inch round cake pans. Line the bottoms of the pans with circles of baking parchment or waxed paper. Dust the sides of the pans with flour and tap out the excess. In a microwave-safe bowl, melt the chocolate on high for 1 to 2 minutes, or until melted, stirring halfway through cooking. Set the chocolate aside to cool to room temperature for 10 minutes.

In a large bowl, stir the flour, baking powder, and salt. In another large bowl, using a handheld electric mixer, beat the butter and sugar until combined. Beat in the melted chocolate and vanilla extract. One at a time, add the eggs, beating well after each addition. Add the flour mixture and milk in thirds, beating until just combined. Scrape the batter into the prepared pans and spread evenly. Bake for 25 to 30 minutes, or until a toothpick inserted in the center of each layer comes out clean. Transfer the pans to a wire rack. Cool 10 minutes. Carefully invert the cake layers onto the rack and cool completely.

Place one layer on a serving plate. Spread frosting over the cake and top with the second cake layer. Frost the outside of the cake, then the top. Store in the refrigerator. Serves 12.

Cubcakes:

To make pawprint cupcakes, bake the Chocolate Celebration Cake in two 12-cup muffin tins for 20 minutes. Frost the cupcakes with white icing (for a furry paw, mix the frosting with grated coconut first). Top each cupcake with a small mint patty. Then place three Junior Mints or chocolate chips around the patty for claw marks. Beware — cubcakes walk away fast. Makes 24.

FamilyFun COOKING

Better-Than-Basic Yellow Cake

Although it certainly is easier to reach for a cake mix, all the ingredients for this moist yellow cake are in your pantry. Try it — it's worth the effort.

- 4 eggs, separated
- 2¾ cups all-purpose flour
- 1½ teaspoons baking powder
- ½ teaspoon salt
- 1 cup butter, softened
- 2 cups sugar
- 2 teaspoons vanilla extract
- 1 cup milk

Lightly grease and dust with flour two 9-inch round cake pans, or one 13- by 9- by 2-inch pan. Preheat the oven to 350°. Using an electric mixer, beat the egg whites until stiff, but not too dry, and set aside. Sift the flour along with the baking powder and salt.

In a large bowl, cream the butter, gradually pouring in the sugar, beating until the mixture is fluffy. Beat in the egg yolks, one at a time. Add the vanilla extract and continue to beat.

Using a spatula or wooden spoon, add the flour mixture to the butter mixture in three additions, alternating with the milk. Fold the egg whites gently and thoroughly into the batter.

Pour the batter into the baking pan(s), spreading it out with a spatula. Bake the rounds for 35 to 40 minutes and the rectangle for 40 to 50 minutes, or until a toothpick inserted in the middle comes out clean. Cool in the pan for 5 minutes before inverting onto a wire rack to cool completely. Serves 10.

Hopscotch Cake:

Follow the Better-Than-Basic directions for a 13- by 9- by 2-inch cake. Once cooled, cut the cake into eight equal rectangular pieces. Arrange the pieces on a board or serving tray in the classic hopscotch pattern (see diagram at right). Use about 2 cups of frosting to ice the cake. Decorate each rectangle with snipped licorice strings, shredded coconut, colored crystal sugars, or rainbow sprinkles. Make numbers with candies, raisins, peanuts, or pieces of fruit leather. Then let your kids take turns standing a short way from the cake and tossing a piece of candy or cereal onto it. The "tosser" gets to eat the slice of cake on which his marker lands.

Hopscotch Cake

How To Grease Cake Pans

☛ For an easy flip out of the pan, grease your cake pans (bottom and sides) with shortening — not butter — and then dust with flour.

Can I Have Dessert?

Also from FamilyFun magazine

* **FamilyFun magazine:** a creative guide to all the great things families can do together. Call 800-289-4849 for a subscription.

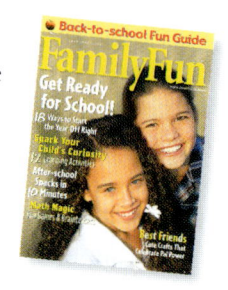

* **FamilyFun Cookbook:** a collection of more than 250 irresistible recipes for you and your kids, from healthy snacks to birthday cakes to dinners everyone in the family can enjoy (Disney Editions, $24.95). The recipes in *FamilyFun Cooking* are excerpted from this book.

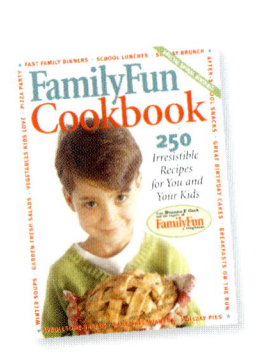

* **FamilyFun Crafts:** a step-by-step guide to more than 500 of the best crafts and activities to do with your kids (Disney Editions, $24.95).

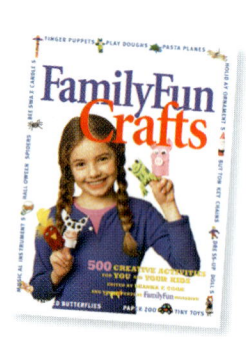

* **FamilyFun Parties:** a complete party planner featuring 100 celebrations for birthdays, holidays, and every day (Disney Editions, $24.95).

* **FamilyFun Cookies for Christmas:** a batch of 50 recipes for creative holiday treats (Disney Editions, $9.95).

* **FamilyFun Tricks and Treats:** a collection of wickedly easy crafts, costumes, party plans, and recipes for Halloween (Disney Editions, $14.95).

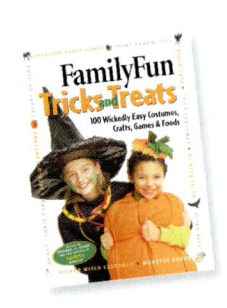

* **FamilyFun.com:** visit us at www.familyfun.com and search our extensive archives for games, crafts, recipes, and other boredom-busting activities.

Photography Credits

Special thanks to the following *FamilyFun* magazine photographers for their excellent work.

Robert Benson: 42

Michael Carroll: 11; 44; 45

Alan Epstein: 9 (top); 10;

Tom Hopkins: 17 (top left); 18; 20 (bottom); 28; 29; 31 (top); 32; 34; 35 (top); 40 (top); 46 (top)

Brian Leatart: 13; 19; 20 (top); 26; 39

Lightworks Photographic: 3; 4; 5; 6; 7; 8; 9 (bottom); 12 (bottom); 14 (bottom); 15 (top right); 16 (bottom); 21; 22; 23; 24; 25; 27; 30; 31 (bottom); 33; 36; 37; 38; 40 (bottom); 41; 43; 46 (bottom)

Steven Mark Needham: 16 (top)

Joanne Schmaltz: 47

Shaffer/Smith Photography: 17 (top right, middle, bottom); 35 (bottom)

Chip Yates: 15 (top left)